leapfrog

The Bossy Cockerel

First published in 2000
Franklin Watts
96 Leonard Street
London
EC2A 4XD

Franklin Watts Australia
45-51 Huntley Street
Alexandria
NSW 2015

A CIP catalogue record for this book is available
from the British Library.

ISBN 0 7496 3708 0 (hbk)
ISBN 0 7496 3828 1 (pbk)

Series Editor: Louise John
Series Advisor: Dr Barrie Wade
Series Designer: Jason Anscomb

Printed in Hong Kong

The Bossy Cockerel

by Margaret Nash

Illustrated by Elisabeth Moseng

W
FRANKLIN WATTS
LONDON•SYDNEY

Charlie the Cockerel was handsome, but he was also very bossy!

"Cock-a-doodle-doo!"

"Get me this, get me that,"
he said to the hens.

The hens were getting
fed up.

Charlie was far too big
for his boots.

The hens left one by one.

They began scratching in a new patch of ground.

Suddenly, Hattie the Hen
flapped her wings.

"There's something buried
over here!" she said.

"What is it?" clucked
the other hens.

Charlie flew over to have a look.

The hens scratched wildly.
Dust flew everywhere ...

... high up in the air, and straight into Charlie's face!

"Stop!" spluttered Charlie. "It's only a rusty, old bird!"

"Silly, ugly, metal thing."

The hens were very
disappointed.

They had their dust baths
and went to bed.

The next morning, they all got a surprise.

The farmer had put the metal bird on the roof. It was gold and shiny.

Charlie flew onto the roof.
"Go away!" he cried.

But the bird didn't speak.

Suddenly, the bird
turned in the wind.

It knocked Charlie
right off the roof!

The hens laughed until their feathers shook.

"Charlie won't be able to boss *him* around," chuckled Hattie the Hen.

And she was right!

Leapfrog has been specially designed to fit the requirements of the National Literacy Strategy. It offers real books for beginning readers by top authors and illustrators.

There are 25 Leapfrog stories to choose from: